ABOUT THE BANK STREET READY

More than seventy-five years of education, teaching, and quality publishing have earned The Bank Street College of Education its reputation as America's most trusted name in early childhood education.

Because no two children are exactly alike in their development, the Bank Street Ready-to-Read series is written on three levels to accommodate the individual stages of reading readiness of children ages three through eight.

● *Level 1:* GETTING READY TO READ (Pre-K–Grade 1)
Level 1 books are perfect for reading aloud with children who are getting ready to read or just starting to read words or phrases. These books feature large type, repetition, and simple sentences.

● *Level 2:* READING TOGETHER (Grades 1–3)
These books have slightly smaller type and longer sentences. They are ideal for children beginning to read by themselves who may need help.

○ *Level 3:* I CAN READ IT MYSELF (Grades 2–3)
These stories are just right for children who can read independently. They offer more complex and challenging stories and sentences.

All three levels of The Bank Street Ready-to-Read books make it easy to select the books most appropriate for your child's development and enable him or her to grow with the series step by step. The levels purposely overlap to reinforce skills and further encourage reading.

We feel that making reading fun is the single most important thing anyone can do to help children become good readers. We hope you will become part of Bank Street's long tradition of learning through sharing.

The Bank Street College
of Education

To my grandson, Willy
—D.O.
For Simon
—J.D.

THE SPAGHETTI PARTY
A Bantam Book/March 1995

Published by Bantam Doubleday Dell Books
for Young Readers, a division of Bantam
Doubleday Dell Publishing Group, Inc.
1540 Broadway, New York, New York 10036.

Special thanks to Susan Schwarzchild,
Matt Hickey, Hope Innelli, and Kathy Huck.

The trademarks "Bantam Books" and the
portrayal of a rooster are registered
in the U.S. Patent and Trademark Office
and in other countries. Marca Registrada.

Library of Congress Cataloging-in-Publication Data
Orgel, Doris.
The spaghetti party / by Doris Orgel ;
illustrated by Julie Durrell.
p. cm. — (Bank Street ready-to-read)
"A Byron Preiss book."
Summary: Annie tells her friends to "come as you are"
—and they do!
ISBN 0-553-09052-6 (hardcover). — ISBN 0-553-37571-7 (pbk.)
[1. Play—Fiction. 2. Parties—Fiction.]
I. Durrell, Julie, ill. II. Title. III. Series.
PZ7.0632Sp 1995
[E]—dc20
94-9788   CIP   AC

Published simultaneously in the United States and Canada

PRINTED IN THE UNITED STATES OF AMERICA

0 9 8 7 6 5 4 3 2 1

The Spaghetti Party

by Doris Orgel
Illustrated by Julie Durrell

A Byron Preiss Book

BANTAM BOOKS
NEW YORK • TORONTO • LONDON • SYDNEY • AUCKLAND

One sunny Sunday
Annie called up her friend Keesha.
"Hi, Keesha, want to come play?"
But Keesha said, "Lori's here.
We're cooking spaghetti and meatballs.

We're a mess!"
"That's okay," said Annie.
"Just COME AS YOU ARE!"
"Well, maybe when we're done,"
Keesha said and hung up.

Annie went up to the attic.
She could have fun there alone.
She opened up a big old trunk.

It was full of dress-up stuff —
a flowered hat, high heels with glitter,
a snorkel, even a crown.
"Let's see, who can I be?"

Meantime, Keesha asked Lori,
"Want to go to Annie's house?"
Lori burst out laughing.
"We're all spotted and spattered!
We have sauce on our noses
and spaghetti in our hair."
But Keesha answered, "That's okay.
Annie said COME AS YOU ARE!"

So they took the spaghetti
and all twenty-seven meatballs
and headed for Annie's house.
On the way they saw Carmela and Luis
giving their dog Potico a bath.

"Hey, Keesha! Hey, Lori!
Where are you going?" Carmela called.
"To Annie's house," they answered.
"Want to come?"

"Yes, let's go!" Luis shouted.
But Carmela said, "No, we can't.
We're all sopping and sudsy!"

"Yes, you can," called Lori and Keesha.
"Annie said COME AS YOU ARE!"
So Carmela and Luis came along.
Potico came, too,
with his favorite Frisbee.

On the way to Annie's,
they saw Ben and Buzzy.
"Where are you going?" yelled Ben.
"To Annie's house," said Luis.

"Want to come?" called Carmela.
"But we're all silver and sloshy,"
said Buzzy.

"That's okay," said everyone.
"Annie said COME AS YOU ARE!"
So Ben and Buzzy came along
with their paint and brushes.
"Mmm, I smell something good,"
said Ben.

"I see space guys!" Luis yelled.
Potico barked.
"It's us, Gary and Max," they yelled back.
"Where are you earthlings going?"

"To Annie's house," they all answered.
"Want to come?"
"All the way from Mars?" asked Gary.
"In space suits and goggles?"

And everyone answered, "Yes!
Annie said COME AS YOU ARE!"
So Gary and Max came along,
bringing their space flag.

And they all went together
just exactly as they were:
spotted and spattered,
sopping and sudsy,

silver and sloshy,
in space suits with goggles—
off to Annie's house.

Keesha rang the bell, and
Annie's mom opened the door.
"Annie, come down!" she called.
"Your friends are here!"

"I can't," called Annie.
"I look too funny."

"No fair, you have to!"
shouted all her friends.
"You *said* COME AS YOU ARE!"

So,
very slowly,
flip,
flop,
Annie started down the stairs.
She was sure her friends would
laugh when they saw her.

They all stared.
No one said a word.
Then Luis said,
"Cool, a frog princess!"
Then everyone shouted,
"Annie, you look great!"
And then the party began.

First they played
Frog Princess Meets Space Guys.

Then they painted silver moons
and stars on the fence.

Then they flew to Mars
in Annie's playhouse.

Then they flew back.
"I'm hungry," said Max.
"Me, too!" Gary shouted.

So they ate up all the spaghetti

and all twenty-seven meatballs—yum!

"Let's have another spaghetti
party soon," said Annie.
"Yes!" her friends shouted.
"And we'll all just COME AS WE ARE!"